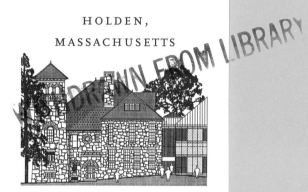

Goodbye to Griffith Street

Story by Marilynn Reynolds
Illustrations by Renné Benoit

ORCA BOOK PUBLISHERS

Griffith Street sat at the foot of the mine where the miners' small, neat houses lined up from one end of the block to the other. John and his mother and father lived in the white house at the end, close to the slag heap.

Night and day, in winter and in summer, the tall smoking chimneys of the mine watched over Griffith Street like kindly giants.

Early every morning, late every afternoon and in the middle of the night, the fathers from Griffith Street carried their black metal lunch pails to work in the mine. Deep underground, the miners dug out nickel and silver. And when they poured hot melted rock onto the slag heap, the sky above Griffith Street turned red as fire.

But John and Mother were moving away from Griffith Street. Their suitcases were packed. Tomorrow, a taxi would take them to the train station and the train would take them to live in a new town. Daddy would be left alone in the white house at the end of the block.

"My mom and dad are getting a divorce and I'm moving away tomorrow," John told his friend Milo from up the street. "Mom says I should say goodbye to you." Milo looked puzzled.

"My mom and I are moving to a new town," John told the Beatle Bugs, Lurlene, Brenda and Andrew Beatle. His friends looked away and went on with their games.

"Goodbye," John said to the smokestacks high above the houses. "Goodbye" to the slag heap where he used to play with the strange twisted shapes of rock.

He wrote his name on the sidewalk with a piece of chalk.

Before Daddy left for work that night, he tucked John into bed and held him for a long time.

"Goodbye, son," he whispered. "I won't be home from work when you and Mom leave in the morning, but I'll visit you often in your new house. We'll still do things together. We'll see each other a lot."

After Dad left, John lay awake and looked around his room. At the pictures on the walls. The curtains on the window. The linoleum floor covered with roses. Goodbye, he thought before he fell asleep.

As John slept, it began to snow.

Flakes of snow drifted down onto the smokestacks of the mine, onto the slag heap, onto the roofs of the miners' houses and onto the streets. Like the whitest, softest blanket in the world, snow covered the town.

John awoke with a start. He sat up. His room was dark and silent. This morning the taxi would come to take him and Mother away. He lifted the window blind. Outside his window, Griffith Street lay still beneath the streetlight. It was covered with snow. Snow!

John tiptoed out to the living room where Mother was asleep on the couch. "It snowed last night and I want to go out," he whispered.

"But it's too early to get up," Mother said.

"I want to say goodbye to the street," John said.

Mother looked at his earnest face. "All right," she said. "Put on your coat and boots. And don't go far away."

John stood on the front steps.

Ever since he was small he'd wanted to be the first to make his mark in the snow. This was the magic morning. The snow lay before him, untouched, waiting.

He breathed in the icy smell of it, took a handful and tasted it. John raised his face. Beautiful snowflakes melted on his forehead and cheeks and eyelids.

What mark would he make? Where would he go first? John took a deep breath.

He stepped into the snow and took giant strides to the house next door where his favorite friend, old Mrs. Wright, lived. Mrs. Wright always let him help her make tomato soup, and she had knitted his best pair of gray mittens. He liked to pet her sturdy little black dog, Queenie.

He wanted to give them a present, and suddenly he had an idea. John went into Mrs. Wright's garden and lay down on the snow. It was the softest thing he'd ever felt. Slowly, carefully, he swung his arms and legs back and forth.

He stood up and stepped away. There, in the snow, lay an angel. Three paces away, he stepped a small circle in the snow and made a star. John smiled. He'd done it. An angel for Mrs. Wright and a star for her little black dog, Queenie.

From Mrs. Wright's house, John took more giant steps until he came to his friend Milo Petrovich's house. He thought about Milo, with his blond straight hair above his blue eyes. He thought about Milo's mother, who couldn't speak English and always wore a babushka over her head. She let John and Milo bounce on her high feather bed and eat cucumbers and carrots from her garden.

Lying down in the snow, he made an angel for Milo and an angel for Milo's mother.

More giant steps across the street to Kathryn Scanlon's house under the streetlight. Kathryn was just a little girl, younger than he was, but he still liked to play with her and teach her how to color in her coloring book. Beside the streetlight he lay down in the snow and made an angel for Kathryn Scanlon and a star for her baby brother who died last year.

John was beginning to feel cold. There was snow in his boots, and his wool mittens were matted and stiff. But he made more giant steps in the snow, past the house of someone he didn't know, to the Beatles' house.

The blue house with the sagging front porch was the home of the Beatle Bugs—Lurlene, Brenda and Andrew Beatle, each with red hair and a freckled face. Sometimes they fought, but most of the time they were friends. Stepping carefully, John made three big stars in the snow right in front of their house.

More giant steps across the street and he was back in front of his own house. The lights were on inside and he saw Mother in her old dressing gown making coffee in the kitchen. The suitcases were sitting on the front step, waiting for the taxi that would take them away.

These have to be the best angels of all, John thought as he lay down again in the snow. He made two angels. One for Mother. One for Daddy. The angels were close together, almost touching. But not touching.

John stood up. It had stopped snowing. He shivered inside his winter coat, but he felt happy.

The streetlight went out, and all along Griffith Street lights began to come on in the miners' houses.

Behind the mine, the winter sun rose weak and distant. Slowly, the sky turned white as the sun lit up the tall smokestacks. It shone its pale light on the slag heap and glanced off the windows of the little houses. It fell on the suitcases sitting on the front steps of the white house at the end of the block.

Soon the morning sun lighted all of Griffith Street.
Griffith Street, covered with angels and stars.

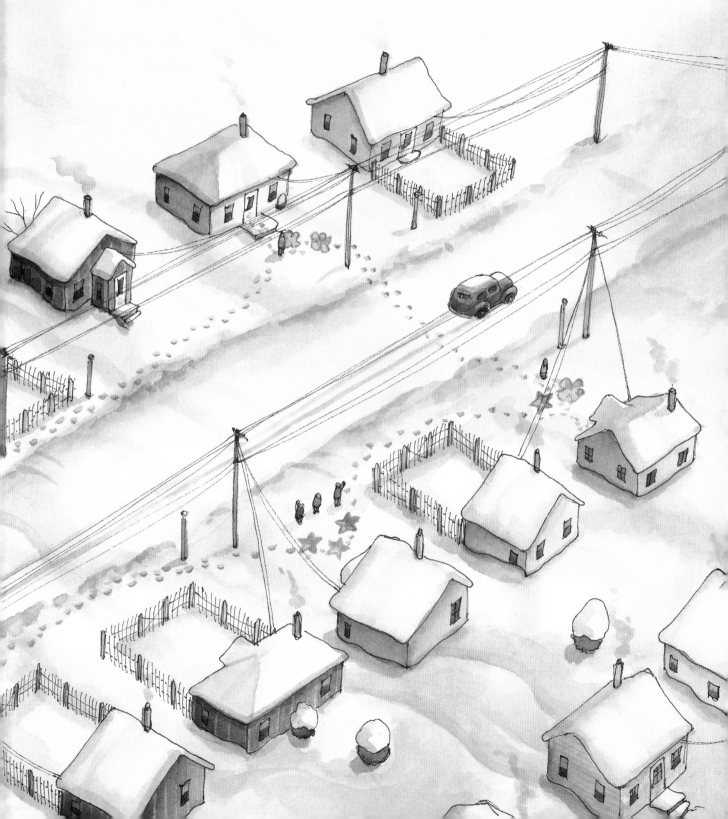